COLLEGE REUNION

CAMPUS
good girl

HALLIE BENNETT

Copyright © 2022 by The Arrowed Heart

BOOKS BY THIS AUTHOR

For those of us who overthink past interactions and dream of what could have been.

PROLOGUE

EMILY

The cafeteria buzzes with a hive of activity as students rush to snag a quick snack before class, while others settle down for a meal with their friends. Finding an empty table for myself, I pour a drop of sanitizer on my hands before digging into lunch, contemplating how much I've grown in my four years at Trinity College.

As a hermit my freshman year, sitting alone in the cafeteria would have been my worst nightmare. Embarrassment would've forced me to grab a to-go box and escape to my dorm room.

But senior Emily is more comfortable in her skin—mostly.

At least you're not a hermit anymore.

Another wave of students enters the small cafeteria, and the volume increases exponentially with raucous laughter and friendly conversations. It won't be long before a scene like this becomes a memory, since graduation is in a few short months.

Sadness dampens my spirit at the coming loss of safety and security college has provided. It's been a bubble of peace in an otherwise drama-filled life.

Don't go there.

Not ready to contemplate life and all its challenges after college quite yet, I focus on eating my turkey sandwich until the chair next to me is drawn back and someone sits down. A whiff of something spicy tickles my nose, and it's a struggle to maintain my composure as this stranger's All-American good looks sink in, making bottle rockets out of my nerves.

Careful not to choke on the bite of lunch in my mouth, I slowly chew and swallow, frantically searching for a reason he'd sit next to me. We're a small, private college with a student body of three hundred people, so I recognize him as a basketball player—though his name escapes me—but I doubt I've registered on his radar before now.

"Hey, I'm Landon." Tan, muscular arms cross over the tabletop as he leans forward, and his charming smile short-circuits rational thought.

Introduce yourself!

"Um, I'm Emily…" Confusion draws the sentence out, and a blush flames to the surface of my skin. *Darn it.* Just when I'm feeling confident about the growth I've made, here comes reality to show me how far I still have to go.

Because my ability to talk to attractive guys? Not great.

Boys who are in relationships or don't trigger a physical reaction? I'm perfectly capable of having intelligent conversation with.

But Landon? He's freaking hot. And I'm not equipped for this, especially when it's so out of the blue.

A laugh comes from the table next to us where more basketball players congregate, watching our by-play with amusement. Landon glances over at them with a shake of his head, then turns back to me. "I didn't want you sitting alone, so I thought I'd join you."

Is this a joke?

His friends are laughing. He doesn't have food to eat. He just plopped down next to me out of the kindness of his heart? When we've never talked before today?

Logic wars with hope. This could be the start of something. Maybe he actually wants to get to know me, and this is his excuse. But then I hear his friends loudly goofing off in the background, obviously making fun of him... or me, and I can't shake the fear that this is some sort of bet he lost.

Take pity on the quiet girl.

Flirt with the chubby nerd.

Like a storyline plucked from a nineties teen movie, except we're not going to fall in love in the end.

Rachel, a girl from my chemistry class, drops her things off in a chair, her gaze bouncing between the two of us, before getting in line for slices of pizza, and the presence of a witness to whatever the heck he's doing must unnerve him. He fidgets in his seat for a second—*probably wondering if he should continue this farce*—before standing up with a jerk of his chair.

"Oh, it looks like you've got someone already." Right as he finishes his sentence, Kelly and Melanie take seats across from us, and he quickly excuses himself. But instead of heading to the table of basketball players, he leaves the cafeteria altogether. Another round of amusement erupts from his teammates next door.

Curiouser and curiouser.

"What was that about?" Kelly asks, all three of us tracking Landon's movements until he disappears from sight.

"I have no clue. He said he didn't want me sitting alone."

"That's nice..." Bewilderment creases Kelly's brow. "But wasn't that Landon Greer? Nice isn't how I would describe him."

"Yeah, I'd say he's more of a *friendly* type of guy." Melanie's eyebrows wiggle with insinuation, but she must read my ignorance because she explains, "I overheard one cheerleader bragging about their night together, then her friend chimed in to confirm his sexual talent. Seems the entire squad has either slept with him or plans on it."

Unerringly, my eyes drift to the side where a couple of those girls have joined the basketball team. While they're covered in sweats or jeans rather than cute cheerleading uniforms, underneath the thick outer layers are toned muscles and lithe curves from all their workouts—a complete opposite to my "college fifteen" weight gain.

More like college twenty-five.

And I immediately dismiss the whisper of *What if?* that taunted me when Landon appeared. Why would he want me when he has cheerleaders vying for his attention?

This was a fluke occurrence—a game between him and his friends—and I bet he forgets about me before the day is done.

CHAPTER ONE

LANDON
TEN YEARS LATER

"Hey, look who's here." My buddy Josh motions to the doorway with his drink, and I see two women enter the room—both beautiful in short cocktail dresses, but only one snares my attention like a hound on the hunt.

Emily Houghton.

It's been ten years since I last saw her on the day of our graduation, and she's as gorgeous as ever. Even more so with fuller curves and a glow about her that only comes with maturity.

For a decade, I've worked to get my life together—blazed through a string of superficial relationships—yet Emily remained in the back of my mind, a beacon of what could be.

I wouldn't call it pining exactly.

We've never spoken more than a few words to each other. But my deepest fantasy of claiming the good girl—making her mine in the filthiest of ways, of basking in her aura of warmth and kindness—it followed me into every one-night-stand or doomed-to-fail relationship.

"Are you finally going to do something about this crush of yours? Or are you going to wait another decade before growing a pair of balls?" Josh asks with a smirk, and a couple of our former teammates snicker. It's no secret I was gone for Emily our senior year, but I didn't realize they knew about my lingering infatuation.

Taking a measured drink of my cocktail—some specially made fruity concoction Josh forced us to try—I consider my options. Wasting another chunk of my life wondering *What if?* isn't appealing. Better to get it out of my system. Except I'm not convinced a weekend with Emily will be enough. What if the experience of knowing what it's like to have her only heightens my obsession?

We live worlds apart.

Do I expect us to start a relationship?

Hell, she could already be in one.

A jealous knot coils around my heart as I search for any sign Emily arrived with someone other than her friend. No man hanging around in the background, though that hardly comforts me. He could be parking the car or in the restroom. The tart flavor of pineapple burns my tongue as I swig the rest of my cocktail in one go. I don't want her to have a man.

And if she doesn't? What are you going to do about it?

This is our ten-year reunion.

Homecoming weekend.

Our time's limited, and while I've never had a problem getting women, Emily's different. She makes *me* feel different. Case in point? The one and only time I approached her in college and confused the hell out of her. That awkward five minutes during lunch replays in my dreams, remembering her scrunched brows, the hesitancy in her voice. I lost any sort of flirting skills I possessed the moment I sat next to her.

"I'm not sure yet. I didn't come here with plans to make a move." Not entirely true, but a course of action eludes me.

The guys share looks of doubt when the Dean of Student Alumni calls for everyone's attention and ushers us into a larger room set up for the banquet dinner. Cocktail hour's over, and any chance I had to casually approach Emily ends with it.

I try to focus as conversations swirl around me from players and their significant others, smiling and nodding at each introduction and life update like my every cell isn't honed into the fact that Emily is in my line of vision. She keeps checking her phone, a frown pinching her bow-shaped lips, and I wonder what's wrong.

Who's on the other end of the line? A husband? A boyfriend?

Whoever they are, the exchange doesn't improve the longer the evening wears on because Emily visibly wilts as each hour passes—shoulders drooping, smiles dimming. I wish I could check on her, but I doubt a stranger digging into her private life is what she needs right now.

Her friends are probably better equipped to help her, anyway.

But they seem distracted by talking amongst themselves. Can't they see how disengaged she is from their conversation? Why isn't someone saying something?

"Earth to Landon!" A hard punch lands on my arm, jolting me back to awareness. Varying degrees of amused and annoyed expressions greet me as my eyes pan around the table. Michael, the offended party, waves his hand in front of my face. "Can you forget about Emily for a second? Considering how we were roommates for two years while you've only spoken two sentences to her? I asked what you thought about the Pacers trading Madison for Young."

Normally, discussing basketball news would excite me, but it pisses me off he wants to cop an attitude because I missed a random question. "I thought it was a shitty move. Satisfied?"

"Easy, boys." Josh's wife intercedes, raising her hands in a mock stance of holding us away from each other. "Landon, it's rude to ignore your friends, even if it is to stare longingly at the woman of your dreams. And Michael, lighten up. The four of us literally had dinner together last weekend where y'all debated this same topic."

Everyone grins at her expert wrangling. As if we're the age of her and Josh's little girl.

Michael and I shrug in agreement, and the mood brightens with easier conversation that I try making a priority, instead of spying on Emily every two seconds.

Every five seconds is good, though, right?

CHAPTER TWO

EMILY

My phone remains blessedly silent after a night of fielding urgent messages from my parents requesting money. *Requesting.* A dark chuckle interrupts the silence in my hotel room as I get ready for a morning of leading campus tours for alumni. *That's putting it nicely—demanding would be more apt.*

Sighing, I tug my unruly curls into a ponytail and lament my family circumstances. *Can't even have one weekend to myself.* One weekend where I can be worry-free, without being pestered for cash.

Unbidden, the last conversation I had with my best friend before arriving echoes in my mind.

"I don't think I should go."

"What are you talking about? We've been planning this trip for months." Melanie groans on the other end of the phone, her frustration palpable.

"I know, but it doesn't seem wise to spend so much money for one weekend when I already have so many other expenses here." My computer screen scrolls down the budget I'm reevaluating for the umpteenth time as if suddenly the bevy of bills—mine and my parents'—will magically disappear.

"You don't want to get me started on those other expenses, Emily," she warns. *"We're going to the reunion, and we're going*

to have fun. You deserve time for yourself to relax, and it's your fucking money. If you want to splurge on a weekend getaway to see old college friends, then that's your right."

All things she'd said before. Things I'd told myself countless times.

Yet I couldn't shake the anxious worry. What if something went wrong while I was away?

And lo-and-behold, my pessimistic prediction came true.

The battery went out on my dad's car, so he needed cash for a new one or else he wouldn't be able to pick my sister up from her friend's sleepover the next day. Of course, there were a flurry of texts stressing the time-constraint—not allowing for any other possibilities to be suggested.

What if her friend's mom dropped her off at home?

Well, we're going to need to drive the car sometime.

Your disability check comes in tomorrow. Why can't it wait until then?

We need that money for bills. Are you going to help us or not?

Except "bills" probably meant my mom using the money on a night out with her girlfriends while the electric and car insurance amounts due would rack up another round of late fees. I try not to begrudge her an evening of fun considering the otherwise sad state of our family, but it's disheartening when she takes my dad's disability check for her own because she refuses to get a job—listing one excuse after another on why she can't work.

Which leaves me to pick up the slack if I want to be a "good daughter".

A thin film of tears forms before I blink it away.

I don't have time to wallow in self-pity. I'm saving that for my last night here before heading home to deal with all my family drama. The same drama that plagued me when I attended Trinity College years ago. In many ways, I've grown since then, but the glaring pit in my life—the one I can't escape no matter how hard I try—is stuck firmly in place.

My dramatic, irresponsible family.

Rapid knocking pounds on the hotel door before Melanie walks in with a box full of donuts and two iced coffees. She'd met with her old mentor this morning for breakfast, and I'm happy to see she brought some back with her.

And to have a distraction from my maudlin thoughts.

"How's Mrs. Chalk?" Snagging my coffee and a sprinkled donut, I devour the sugary sweetness before sitting on the bed to put on my sneakers. Today's activities call for comfortability, which means tennis shoes, stretch capris, and a short sleeve tee the college gave out to alumni volunteers.

"Good. Enjoying her retirement." Melanie flops onto the other bed in the room, then shakes her head at the emblazoned VOLUNTEER printed on the back of my shirt. "I can't believe you agreed to spend your day walking people around campus when they could easily do it themselves. We're all grown-ups, you know."

"Yes, but someone needs to point out new improvements or renovations while keeping visitors occupied. Besides, it's not all day, just an hour or so. No big deal." I shrug, grabbing my small purse and slinging it across my chest. "I used to do this stuff all the time as a member of the Student Activities Council. That's why Kenzie asked me. She knew she could trust me to do a good job since I've already done it before."

"They still should have gotten current students to do the grunt work. Everyone's already here for Homecoming. It wouldn't have been that hard." Melanie pushes as we hop into my car and drive the short three miles to campus. Letting current students lead would've provided an excellent learning opportunity to enhance their public speaking skills, but I'm not too upset with filling in for them.

I can use the distraction to distance myself from the headache of last night. The same kind of distraction I used a decade ago when avoiding the stress of my family.

Some things never change.

After parking near the center of campus, we agree to meet up later before going our separate ways—Melanie to join the volleyball team for a recreational alumni game while I head to the admissions office for instructions. It's been a few years since I've been on campus, but this old building looks the same. Creaking with age, smelling of dust and textbooks, nostalgia settles over me like a cozy blanket, and I'm transported back to a simpler time in my life.

Funny how confident I used to be that if I just graduated, if I just got a good enough job, then my life—and correspondingly, my family's—would get better.

Instead, my problems stayed the same despite a nice job with benefits. Every perk for quality work, every promotion, materialized into giving more to my family. Nothing was ever enough.

Still isn't enough.

It's like I can never get ahead, no matter how hard I try.

Thought we were saving self-pity and depression for Sunday night.

Right. Time to put on a happy face.

A group of five people stands in front of the admissions office, and I recognize Kenzie as one of them. Our friendship has lasted over a decade after meeting freshman year during a class picnic, and its endurance can be attributed to the odd connection we share. Unlike most of my friend group, we rarely talk to each other—no texts or video chats and definitely nothing in-person since we live states apart—but every once in a while, one of us will call the other, and we'll catch up like no time has passed.

We understand each other in a way that's difficult to describe, but it works for us.

Because she doesn't only talk to you when she needs something. She calls just because she's interested in hearing about your life.

Kenzie smiles and waves when she sees me, then starts explaining everyone's tasks for the day. I see Kyle in the group and wonder how she's handling having her ex-boyfriend present. I know there are no hard feelings between the two, but it can't be easy being tossed back into a familiar setting where you once were voted as one of the school's power couples in the yearbook.

"Emily, your tour starts in the Henley Arts Center at nine-thirty." Kenzie hands me a sheet of paper with a highlighted route and tidbits of information sprinkled throughout, and I begin the trek across campus to Henley. With only ten buildings, including dorms to its name, Trinity College's tiny campus is quaint and beautifully maintained, mature oaks and flowering shrubs lining sidewalks.

I loved living on campus as a student. It provided a safe oasis away from my home life, and at one point, I considered staying after graduation—getting a position in admissions so I could enjoy more of that peace. However, reality, in the form of my family getting evicted, destroyed any thoughts of staying. They needed me at home to help them find a new place to live, to supplement their meager disability income with earnings from waitressing until something better suited to my degree appeared.

The Henley Arts Center housed the auditorium at its central point, while classrooms for choir, drama, and painting lined the hallways on either side of the building. At the north entrance, two couples and a lone man stand chatting, obviously waiting for my arrival, and I appreciate their punctuality. Responsible adults are a refreshing change. Reminds me I'm not the only one in the world who concerns herself with other's feelings.

"Good morning! I'm Emily, and I'll be leading our tour today. Would you all like to introduce yourselves? Then we can get started." Names billow forth without hesitation, ending with a rich baritone from the lone man—Landon Greer.

Grown more handsome with age, I school my expression into one of friendly ambivalence despite the wave of heat spiking my blood. Blonde locks fall in playful layers on his head, begging for a woman's hand to run through it—to smooth and adjust, to tug and hold on to while riding his...

Whoa.

So much for ambivalence.

Turning on my heel, I stammer out a "Follow me" and start the tour, stunned by the physical effect Landon has on me. My breathing's labored. My thighs clench against a burst of arousal.

From just one look?

I realize I felt this way around him in college, too. When he sat next to me at lunch all those years ago, I had a visceral response. It expressed itself through brain fog and blushes, though. Not this intense lust.

I've never met anyone else who's elicited the same reaction. To the point where I've wondered if something's wrong with me, because while I can objectively appreciate attractiveness, my hormones stay in control. They don't fly off the rails, eager to lie beneath a man the moment I'm within range.

Guess I haven't been in the right man's presence.

Until now.

Except nothing can happen between us.

I don't do flings... or really any sort of relationship due to my family.

If there's one thing I'm dead set against, it's bringing someone I love into the mess and drama of my world. The pain and stress it's caused me is enough to last a lifetime, so I won't be responsible for burdening a partner with the same harmful baggage.

It's the main reason I've been alone all these years. And a virgin to boot. Because my stupid emotions won't let me sleep with a stranger, yet those same emotions won't let me truly connect with a person, either. A catch twenty-two resulting in abstinence.

"We heard the school received a donation of half a million dollars last year. Do you know how they're allocating those funds?" The older gentleman of a couple celebrating their thirty-fifth class reunion asks as we pass the newly renovated Giles Men's Dorm. For most of our tour so far, I've been running on autopilot as we walk from building to building, so I'm thankful for the timely interruption. Fears of being alone forever can wait until Sunday night.

Can't wait...

"If you signed up to receive the alumni newsletter, they listed a couple of possibilities: adding another wing to the science building, supporting the growth of a women's wrestling team, or repaving the parking lots since most are showing signs of wear with cracks and potholes." Thank goodness I actually read that particular email. Most times, I dump Trinity's emails in the spam folder, since the majority of their newsletters ask for donations. As if I don't have enough people asking me for money already.

"Those don't seem very exciting. A women's wrestling team?" His wife wrinkles her nose and pats her silver bob with a sniff. "Surely there's not enough interest in such a sport to warrant spending so much money on it."

"You'd be surprised," Landon jumps in, coming to walk beside me, and his sudden proximity makes the sweat from hiking around campus increase tenfold.

Good grief, did his hand brush mine?

"They took a poll in July asking former students and staff what they thought needed the most financial attention. There were a lot of options, and those three won the most votes."

Unconvinced murmurs rumble from the couple, but all I can do is stare at Landon in shock. "You read the school newsletters?"

"Don't you?" he asks with a sly grin, green eyes twinkling in the sunlight.

"Not every single one. I didn't know about the poll."

Landon's tongue makes a clicking sound of mock disapproval, and I'm fascinated by his mouth. Framed by the shadow of a beard, it's full and entirely kissable. Not that I've ever been kissed, but I imagine it would be perfect with him.

"What a shame. I'm guessing you missed the announcement of discontinuing the art magazine? Sadly, Trinity Kaleidoscope will be no more." He sighs as our tour finishes full circle back at the arts center, and the two couples wave goodbye, leaving us alone.

"Are you serious?" The art magazine was a project I helped get off the ground my junior year. It took us hours of preparing budgets and presentations, and now they were canceling it? "Was that one of the points in the list of items to receive donations? Because if I'd have known, I would've voted and... I can't believe all that hard work..."

"Hey, no. I'm sorry. I shouldn't have said that." Landon cups my shoulder and rubs his thumb over the seam of my sleeve. "It was a joke. A dumb one. I knew you were a part of the magazine team, so I..." His head jerks to the side with an awkward clearing of his throat. "I don't know. But I apologize. I didn't mean to freak you out."

My body sags in relief against the brick of the building as Landon adds another hand to my shoulders, lightly massaging them. It's an odd sensation. One I'm not sure how to handle, so instead, I blurt out a question addressing the other part of this conversation that confuses me. "How did you know I worked on the Kaleidoscope?"

"Oh." He takes a step back, and the absence of his touch leaves me cold. *No, it leaves you just as you were—a normal temperature of ninety-eight point two degrees.* "I read an article about the project in the school paper when the first magazine was produced. Your name was mentioned multiple times."

"I'm surprised you remember. Or even read the school paper." Realizing how bad that sounds, I wince and offer my own apology. "Sorry, that came out wrong. I shouldn't stereotype you just because you're an athlete."

"So, you remember me, too, huh?" A brightness returns to his features as he straightens, and the smug satisfaction creasing his eyes and mouth is reminiscent of the young arrogance I remember most of the athletes on campus exuding.

Is he flirting with me?

If he is, it's probably because he flirts with everyone.

Ah, there's reality rearing its ugly head again.

With a brief nod towards the entirety of Trinity College laid out before us, I answer, "Small campus. Hard to forget anyone, even if names don't always accompany recognition."

Good save.

It's not as if my body recalls his or wants more of his touch. Nope. We're only former classmates who happen to know tiny inconsequential facts about the other. That's all. No desire or lust here.

Liar.

CHAPTER THREE

LANDON

O*uch.*

Her words are a blow to my ego, though I guess it's no surprise she barely remembers me. We ran in different circles in college—me with the basketball team and her with the group of do-gooders that professors loved because they never caused trouble.

Me and my friends, on the other hand...

Stuck in a conservative Midwestern town because we took the scholarships Trinity offered us, hoping to eventually transfer to a D1 division school? Well, we raised hell and scraped by in classes, especially once it became clear we didn't possess the talent to play basketball at a higher level. I'd drowned myself in booze and pussy until Coach told me to either shape up or drop out because I was only wasting everyone's time and my parents' money.

"Are you heading to the outdoor obstacle course? It looks like people are gathering over there." Emily points to the quad, where tees emblazoned with Trinity's logo reign supreme. I see Josh's shock of red hair rise above the crowd and remember signing up for the group activity. It's supposed to be a bonding experience to get us off campus for the afternoon, and I glance between my friends and Emily—the choice a no-brainer.

There's only one person I want to *bond* with today.

"Are you going?" I counter, prepared to base my answer off hers. The brief time we've spent together isn't enough; I need more. It was only by sheer luck I ended up in her tour group this morning. Thank God curiosity got the better of me, prompting me to sign up for a campus tour while the rest of my friends slept in.

"No, I agreed to help prepare for Sunday's brunch, so I'll be hanging out at the church for the next few hours." She motions to the idyllic stone church the college is named after, the stained-glass windows decorating its steeple shooting rainbows of color into the air.

Decision made.

"Could you use another hand? I'm free to join you if that's okay." *Please say yes.*

"Are you sure? You don't have to, and the outdoor course sounds fun."

You're not getting rid of me that easily.

"I'd rather spend time with you." There. All my cards on the table. I can't be any clearer than that.

A hint of fall floats on the breeze between us, teasing the ebony curls escaping Emily's braid. God, she really is beautiful. Even in a basic tee and denim. I hope I haven't scared her away with my blunt honesty.

Shades of red and pink blend on her cheeks and neck, and she toys with the folded sheet of paper in her hand, teeth nibbling her bottom lip. "This is going to sound insecure. But this is new to me, so I've got to ask: why? We're strangers to each other despite four years of college together."

"You want to hear all my secrets, huh? Why don't we talk while setting up the brunch?" It'll give her something to focus on other than wearing the paper in her fidgety hands down to scraps. Black ink's already starting to rub off on her fingertips from the incessant folding.

Emily nods—skepticism still narrowing her pretty brown eyes—and ten minutes later, we're wrapping silverware in cloth napkins for Sunday's awards brunch. A few other alumni and students arrange the tables and chairs, but thankfully, we're left to ourselves at a separate table in the back.

"So..." A world of curiosity lives within that one softly spoken word, and I know it's time to come clean about my feelings.

Because Emily's a cautious woman.

Even in college, I recognized the air of hesitancy that surrounded her. Though smart and full of good ideas, in the one class we had together, she rarely raised her hand to answer questions. And the conversations I overheard when we were partnered near each other revealed how concerned she was with following instructions carefully, double-checking each section of work for any mistakes.

Grabbing a fresh napkin and laying it flat before me, I snag a fork, spoon, and knife from the boxes in front of us, deciding to start from the beginning. "It's going to sound like I'm a stalker."

She sets aside a finished silverware set and eyes me from across the table. "You weren't peeping through my dorm window, were you?"

Oh, shit.

"Hell, no." I shake my head vehemently. "Not that stalkerish."

A nervous laugh crops up, and I wish I could rewind the last thirty seconds. What is wrong with me? Women don't usually get inside my head and cause me to blurt out the dumbest shit possible. Yet Emily seems to have a knack for making me flustered as fuck. "One night senior year, I was watching a game in the commons when I looked outside and saw you and your friends running through the rain. For the first time, you became real to me. More than just the reserved girl who never took a misstep. You had a wild streak in you, and I wanted to discover how deep it ran. Plus, it didn't hurt that your tank clung to your breasts like a second skin."

Arousal hardens my cock at the memory, and I shift in my seat. The glow of the streetlight had shimmered across the drops of water on her skin, creating the image of an incandescent water nymph—an innocent little nymph I'd wanted to drink down in one thirsty gulp.

My secret fantasy and obsession merging to center on the tantalizing woman before me.

Emily's gaze widens at my last comment before glancing down at her chest as if to ensure she isn't wearing the revealing tank now instead of a decade ago. "I always wondered if anyone ever noticed us racing through the rain..." An audible exhale fills the space as her words trail off. Then, she licks her lips and pins me with an odd blending of bold and shy as she adds, "And I kind of hoped someone would notice me, dumb as it sounds. All those romantic movie scenes with couples in the rain, I guess."

"So, the good girl admits to her wild side." *Hallelujah!* I knew she had it, but now it feels like we can get on the same page for this weekend—chatting, kissing, *fucking*. The normal progression of whatever this is compressed into a short time span.

A bitter laugh erupts from Emily, her face darkening to match the weary expression she wore last night at the dinner. "Being good isn't all it's cracked up to be."

"What do you mean?"

"I struggle to say no because I don't like disappointing people. Like today, Kenzie asked if I could help set up the brunch, and there wasn't a second of thought before I automatically agreed. I'm a worker bee—reliable and hardworking." She tosses another finished silverware set to our growing collection. Utensils clank together in a jarring melody, mimicking her inner discord.

"Not bad traits to have," I venture. My hand reaches over to cover hers before she accidentally injures herself by reaching for a knife too quickly or getting stabbed by a fork.

"No, but when people see them as your only defining traits, then I think there's a problem. My value relies on what I can do for others. Sometimes it feels like it's the only reason people keep me around: to have me available to do something for them." Her voice catches, the distress emanating from her hunched form a beacon calling for help—calling for me as every protective instinct I possess charges to the forefront.

Emily pulls her hand away and gets up from the table. "Sorry, I shouldn't have unloaded all that on you. It's not fair or kind when we're just getting to know each other." She tugs on the end of her braid while a hand scrunches the fabric over her heart, as if she's shielding herself. "I don't usually bombard people with my personal issues."

Pushing my chair back, I round the table and urge her behind a privacy screen hiding extra carts of dishes and silverware—allowing us to talk without being in full view of other volunteers. "Em, you don't need to apologize. I bet you weren't expecting a guy to confess to a decade-long crush today, yet that didn't stop me from blindsiding you. We're sharing—some may say over-sharing—but unfortunately, we're on a time crunch."

Emily huffs in frustration. "A secret admirer is sweet. My baggage isn't."

"It doesn't have to be." I enclose one of her hands with mine, halting the mauling of her shirt, and draw her chin up with my finger and thumb. She's so much shorter than me that her head drops back in order to meet my determined gaze. "We all have shit we're dealing with, and none of it's pretty or sweet. I've got my fair share, trust me. But when you care for someone, you agree to take on that burden with them—*for* them when it gets too heavy."

It doesn't shock me how willing I am to bear any burden for her. She's been the one that got away, the woman of my dreams, for a decade now, despite the half-assed attempts I've made at other relationships.

Emily's lashes flutter in response, a suspicious gleam shining at the corners of her eyes before disappearing. "You say the right things. Words I've yearned to hear, but you don't know what you're agreeing to. You don't know that I'm *worth* what you'd be getting into." A distraught warble infuses her tone as she pleads with me to understand. "For years, you've held onto a fantasy of a girl, built her up in your mind. There's no way I measure up to her in the few hours we've hung out. Please don't push for something when I'm telling you: you don't want it."

"We're gonna have to work on you unilaterally making decisions for us." Perhaps I shouldn't tease, not during such an emotional moment, but her attempt at protecting me is as adorable as it is infuriating. "I'm a grown man, sweetheart. I'll decide what I can and cannot handle, and when it comes to you? Throw the whole damn luggage cart my way because if there's one thing I'm sure of, it's that you are entirely fucking worth going through hell and back for. Understand?"

"Honestly? No."

"I'll add it to the list of things to work on." Then I do what I've been craving all day—hell, what I've been craving for ten long years—I kiss Emily Houghton. Because I can't let her go another second believing she's not worthy enough to be loved.

Loved.

Christ, I'm in deep.

CHAPTER FOUR

EMILY

Better than sex cake.

B Junior year, my friends and I found a recipe of chocolate, caramel, and cream with a promise in its name to beat sex with its rich goodness. It came as close to orgasmic as I've ever felt from something other than my own hand.

But the soft kisses Landon's peppering in a sweet line to my mouth blow the mere mix of flour and cocoa out of the water. At the first touch of his lips to my cheek, my heart melts into a liquid mess of emotions, a transformation of solid guard walls to mushy vulnerability—a state I've never allowed myself to reach with a man.

He thinks I'm worthy. He wants to share my burdens.

This is too much, too fast.

Yet, so easy.

All I want to do is stay in Landon's arms—trust him—even if it's only for this weekend.

I sigh and lean further into his embrace, enjoying the sensation of being small compared to him, my head barely reaching his shoulders.

"You're gonna give me what I want, aren't you?" Landon whispers, finally arriving at his destination, his mouth hovering over mine, waiting for... consent? Affirmation? Whatever he's searching for is his, because I'm not in the mood to deny him or myself.

"Yes." An intimate flutter springs from the shared breath between us and swoops lower to settle between my thighs, an insistent pulse to match the rhythm beating in my chest.

"Always a good girl..." There's an arrogance in his tone, a smirk hiding behind the swift press of his lips, but instead of annoying me, his confidence heightens my arousal—assures me he knows what he's doing. Since I definitely can't say the same.

Landon's my first kiss.

At thirty-two years old.

But it's worth the wait.

Teasing licks. Coaxing nibbles of his teeth. They invite me to let him in and experience a world of sensuality I've never known. The buzz of volunteers fades into a hazy consciousness, a sliver of awareness hanging onto the edges, but my mind and body are preoccupied by Landon.

His strong body holding mine.

The intoxicating smell of his cologne.

He's the best distraction I've ever had.

Until the shattering of glass scares the heck out of me, and I jump out of his arms like a rabbit on the run.

"Whoa, easy. Someone must've dropped one of the dishes, but we're okay. You're okay." Landon rubs soothing paths over my arms and shoulders, continuing his massage from earlier to calm my nerves.

Squeezing the handful of his shirt in my hands, a tremulous chuckle breaks the tension. "I know. It just surprised me, but that's probably our cue to keep working on the silverware. We're lucky no one's ready for it yet."

"I'd say we're lucky for more than that." He snares my hand and leads me back to our table, pulling my chair out like a true gentleman and waiting for me to sit before settling in his own seat. "After all, I got to kiss the girl I've been crushing on since senior year, and I should warn you that once isn't going to be enough. Pretty sure I'm gonna need a daily dose. Multiple doses."

Blushing, I scoff at his ridiculousness. "It sounds like you have some horrible disease."

"Notify the CDC." Landon glances around the room as if searching for aid before grinning with mischief. "A love bug's roaming around campus, and I'm hoping it's contagious."

Who'd have thought this former playboy basketball player would possess such a cheesy yet dark sense of humor?

Not me.

But it's nice to see a different side to him—a personality that doesn't rely on his looks or athletic ability... or sexual prowess. Just a man flirting with a woman.

And hope emerges beneath the stony rubble of my protective guards, taking root in the softened landscape of my heart. A feeling that grows deeper as Landon and I spend the rest of the afternoon together until he has practice for the alumni basketball game tomorrow. A game he asks me to attend before dropping a kiss on my forehead and heading for the gym.

What am I getting myself into?

THE SQUEAK OF SNEAKERS echoes in the lobby as I enter the athletic building the next day. Landon's basketball game is already well underway, based on the cheering and whistles coming from the gymnasium, and I blame Melanie for my tardiness. She wouldn't let me leave until I told her about everything that happened yesterday again, as if we hadn't spent the night theorizing and dissecting each word, look, and kiss I'd received from Landon.

Edging through the open set of double doors, I linger on the outskirts of the gym, unsure of myself. I don't recognize anyone in the bleachers whenever I steal a quick peek around, and while I'm not opposed to sitting alone, chatting with a friend would be nice—help ease some of the awkwardness stiffening my muscles.

Too bad Melanie had plans with her old study group or else it wouldn't be an issue.

"Hey, you're Emily, right?" A cheerful woman with a toddler in tow stops beside me.

"Um, yes... But I'm not sure you've got the right person—"

"Landon's Emily?" She asks, a friendly twinkle in her blue eyes. The sense of belonging to someone is new, but not unwelcome. I've only ever relied on myself, an independent woman responsible for others—not the other way around.

"Is that how I'm known now?"

"Among the team? Yes, but it's not a negative thing. We're glad he's finally doing something about this crush of his. He's ready for something more stable than his previous relationships. I'm Maggie, by the way, Josh Parker's wife, and this is Alexis." The little girl hiding behind her leg shyly waves, and I return the greeting with an encouraging smile. "Landon asked me to watch out for you, so now we can join the rest of the team WAGS."

A waft of heat sweeps across my cheeks in pleasure, Landon's thoughtful gesture making me feel wanted—like I belong in his world. Following her lead, we hurry across the basketball court sideline to the players' side of the gym, which remains empty except for a small section of people. "I feel really dumb asking because I should know this, but WAGS?"

Maggie laughs. "Wives and girlfriends of sports athletes. Although, there's a couple of husbands and boyfriends, too, but I don't know how that fits into the acronym."

Climbing the bleacher steps, we sit next to a trio splitting their attention between the game and a passel of kids playing beside the bleachers, fielding stray basketballs. It's strange being on this side of things. Though I didn't attend many basketball games during college, when I did, I always sat on the other side of the gym with the general public—the opposite end of the court reserved for people associated with the team and those covering the game for the news.

"Tristan, Lydia, Amber. This is Emily." Everyone welcomes me with knowing smiles, and it amazes me that so many people know about Landon's crush. I wouldn't have pegged him as the type of guy to wear his heart on his sleeve, sharing his emotions freely with others. Granted, this comes from a woman who rarely shares her intimate emotions, even with close friends.

Another item to add to Landon's list of things for us to work on.

Seems like there's a lot I can learn from him.

Easy conversation flows between the four of us as they regale me with tales of Landon and his friends, and the plethora of insight serves as a glimpse into the life he's led for the past decade while giving me a peek at what our future could be together.

I'd have an extended group of friends who clearly love their people, and I'd be one of them if Landon and I enter a serious relationship.

Another benefit for you, but what about Landon?

He'd receive the short end of the stick between us since my family's nothing like this.

The final buzzer blares in the gym, signaling the end of the game. Eighty-one to seventy-seven—an alumni victory over the current student-led team. Maggie and I exchange numbers to keep in touch after I decline her invitation to a late lunch celebration hosted by Coach K, unsure about Landon's plans.

After saying goodbye, I move down to the gym floor and lean against the wall. Painted concrete steadies my back, a refreshing coolness seeping through the cotton tee as my gaze snags on Landon shaking hands with the opposite team, slapping players on the shoulder in a show of good sportsmanship. But his courtesy is the last thing on my mind when his eyes meet mine—a flash of joy lighting up the dark green—and he walks towards me, politely brushing off attempts to stop him.

"Good game," I say absentmindedly, too focused on the gleam of sweat shining on his skin to utter much else. I'm not sure if it's period hormones announcing their coming arrival or the fact that I've been single my entire life, but everything about Landon makes me want to lick him. From the cord of muscles in his neck to the flexing forearms at his sides, it all tempts me to taste and learn what I've been missing. Even his scent—a combination of soap and sweat—doesn't deter me. Shouldn't he smell like dirty old gym socks or something?

Is this like those pheromone tests? Proving we're compatible?

"Thanks, I'm glad you made it. I don't remember seeing you at games during school." He copies my position, turning his back to the wall and standing beside me as we watch family and friends of the teams file out of the gym while players head to the locker room to clean up. Within minutes, it's just us and a janitor running a long broom across the scuffed floorboards.

"Basketball wasn't really my thing."

"Oh?" Landon's brow raises in question and a devilish part of me wants to tease him.

"Yeah, I prefer baseball, honestly. Something about those tight pants..."

There's a beat of silence.

Anticipation.

Then, with a quick snap of his head towards the janitor, whose back is to us, Landon wraps a hand around my wrist and drags me underneath the bleachers a few feet away. The shift from bright fluorescents to dim shadows is disorienting, but I don't have time to adjust before I'm pressed against the wall—the rough texture prickling my cheek—as a wicked whisper tickles my ear.

"Baseball, hmm? Do you need convincing about the superiority of basketball, sweetheart?" One of his hands braces on the wall beside my head while the other drags a curtain of hair away to bare my neck, placing a gentle kiss on the delicate curve. His entire body cages me in, blocking out the slivers of light that reach us, and I shiver at the sensation of being completely surrounded—a tantalizing blur of protection and domination.

"Maybe I could be persuaded..."

Landon grazes his teeth over my skin. A muttered epithet follows. "I want to corrupt you. Dirty you. You've always fascinated me because you're so fucking good. Professors adored you. Other students recognized your light and knew not to mess with you. It's why those baseball pricks could never deserve you.

Why do you think none of my friends ever teased you like the other girls?"

"Because they weren't interested." Then a new reason occurs to me. "Or because they knew you liked me?"

A chuff of amusement vibrates from his chest. "Trust me, there was interest. You were a challenge—a girl whose vibe said *hands off*—a lure to some assholes. I made it clear not to bother you or else."

I'm not sure how I should feel about this revelation. Discovering I had a secret protector but also learning I wasn't entirely to blame for the lack of male interest in school. "You warned guys away from me?"

"Think of it as protection. They weren't good enough for you, and I wanted you for myself." A slow hand lightly circles my neck, urging my head back to meet Landon's glittering gaze in the shadows. "Still want you as mine alone."

Later I'm sure a stern lecture will come to mind, a list of reasons why it's not his job to keep men from me, but at the moment, it's difficult to think clearly. And there's really only one coherent thought I need to voice now. "Except you never made a move, and I spent a lot of nights crying over why nobody wanted me. Why no one ever asked me out. And it's because of you, for my senior year, at least."

He sighs, resting his bristly cheek against mine. "I'm sorry, but I did try once. It was that lunch where you didn't seem interested, then your friends showed up."

"I thought that was a joke. An entire team of boys were laughing behind my back because you were talking to me. What was I supposed to think?"

It's surreal having this conversation trapped against a gym wall, our breaths mingling in the tight space as Landon lowers his head enough so our lips graze with every word spoken. "Fair point. I didn't think it through, and I let my failure stop me from trying again. For ten fucking years. Don't hold it against me now. Please."

The fleeting crack in his composure softens my frustration. We were both young and insecure when it came to each other back then. Just because gossip described a playboy skilled with women didn't mean he never struck out or suffered from doubts.

Reaching a hand back to cup his shadowed jaw, I draw him closer as I rise onto my tiptoes, giving me enough momentum to land a determined kiss. "We'll probably discuss this again, but it's not an unforgivable offense. Perhaps the fact that you're holding me by the throat isn't clear enough."

"I was hoping that was a good sign." He chuckles. "And a perfect way for us to get back on track. As long as you're up for a little mischief?" His embrace tightens at my slight nod, the gentle squeeze at my neck electrifying every nerve ending with lust. "Unbutton your jeans. Roll them and your panties down over this lush ass. I want to see what's been taunting me since following you around campus yesterday."

"You want me to..." I stammer to a halt, a faint alarm threatening to sound in my head. "But anyone can find us."

In our secluded position, I expected to mess around—maybe make out or touch over the clothes. Revealing more skin wasn't exactly in the plan.

Naïve Emily.

"I'm blocking any view of you, don't worry. Obey, and I promise I'll make it worth your while. Remind you how well good girls are rewarded."

Oh my...

Like a fantasy pulled from the depths of my subconscious, Landon's words unlock the praise kink I always figured I had, but never let someone close enough to experience.

Time to let him in.

Be his good girl.

I drown out the fear of getting caught with desire long held at bay, and my hand lowers to heed his command.

CHAPTER FIVE

LANDON

F*uck.*
　　Emily's actually doing it.

After the hiccup of our conversation—another untimely blunder on my part—I wasn't sure how she'd react. But Emily's consent to continue proves her desire matches my own, leaving me as high as a kite with excitement.

The slow slide of denim and cotton is more erotic than any strip show I've seen during bachelor parties, and the final reveal of pale dimpled skin has my cock stretching the limits of my gym shorts. Stroking my hand in reverence over a round cheek, Emily tremors beneath the intimate caress, feeding my need to comfort her while also wringing more of those sensual shudders from her body.

"You're doing so well, sweetheart," I murmur near her ear. "I can't wait to lick every inch of you. Every hill and valley traced by my tongue. Would you like that?"

"Mhmm..." Her head pushes back into my shoulder as the soft moan purrs from her throat, my fingers twitching at the sexy sensation. The trust she's showing me, the privilege she's granting me, brings me to my knees—every cell wants to kneel at her feet and worship her.

Later. Focus on what you can do now.

"I thought you would. Unfortunately, we need more time, so you can be properly savored." Sliding a hand lower to chart the curve of her ass, I slip between thighs restrained by her jeans and sift through damp curls to circle the wet opening of her pussy. "For now, I'm gonna fuck you with my fingers while you play with your pretty little clit. Together we're gonna make you come all over my hand—give me a sweet teaser of what I'll be eating later tonight."

God willing.

"The dance is tonight."

I forgot about the last big event for this homecoming weekend. There's an alumni awards brunch on Sunday, but since I don't know anyone receiving special accolades, I figured I'd skip it to spend more time with friends. Now, I'm thinking it'll be time spent between Emily's thighs—Josh and the rest of the guys will understand.

"Well, if you're up for it, we could attend the dance together for an hour or two before going somewhere else." *Preferably one of our hotel rooms.* I ease two fingers into her slick pussy, loving the immediate clenching of her walls and imagining the tight heat around my cock. With a couple of shallow thrusts, I test her response. She tries to follow my retreating hand, and I feel the graze of her fingertips as she begins to rub her clit between two fingers.

My obedient little good girl.

"You want me to be your date?" She sounds surprised, like the fact that I'm fingering her beneath the gym bleachers, where anyone could find us, means nothing. Like I'm only in this for a quick fuck.

"Hell, yes." I emphasize the point with a sharp twist of my fingers to hit her g-spot and a brief exertion of pressure on her neck. "When are you going to realize I'm not giving you up so easily, Em. Whatever I must do to make things work with you, I'll do. You want me to put it in writing? Done. Need me begging on my knees? No problem. Whatever you need to feel secure, tell me because it's yours."

A frustrated moan answers. "You say the most perfect things, and my mind's so hazy I can't refute your logic. Is this how you normally charm women into your bidding? Get them so high on pleasure they can't think straight?" Her pace quickens on her clit, and I match the increased speed, pumping hard and deep, splitting my focus between listening and getting her off. It's a novel experience that proves how unique Emily is to me—how she brings out another side of me.

"Not usually. But you've always been a special case for me, and frankly, I'm not above using any advantage I have to make you mine." My teeth bite down on her neck in a show of possession. She's going to wear my mark for everyone to see. So she knows I'm not fucking around with her.

Emily doesn't reply as her pussy clamps down on my fingers and a gush of warmth floods my palm. The orgasm rips through her in waves, and I continue to propel her through it by taking over the jerky movement at her clit with firm strokes of my own.

Eventually, her body sags into mine for support, and I nuzzle the love bite I left behind, shifting my hand from her throat to her waist, holding tight to the precious gift she is. "That was good, sweetheart. You did so well... Now, will you please go to the dance with me?" I wasn't kidding about taking advantage. If she's blissed out on dopamine from her orgasm, then I'm going to press my luck by getting her agreement.

"Yes. I'll go with you, persistent man."

Damn straight.

"BIG DATE TONIGHT. ARE you ready for it?" Josh and I meet in the hallway at our hotel before I pick Emily up from her hotel room across the street. The rush of this afternoon is still a vivid memory inflaming my blood, and I can't wait to see her again—to check in after our shared intimacy and just because I like being near her.

"I've been ready for ten fucking years." I joke, adjusting the collar of my shirt where it scratches at my neck. "It all rides on how Emily's feeling."

Josh smiles in genuine happiness for me as Maggie exits their room to join us, their little girl following in a matching yellow dress. Grabbing his wife's hand before leaving, he pats me on the back. "Good luck, man. If it's meant to be, it'll work out."

"Thanks. I hope so." Because I want what he has. After years of avoiding settling down because it never felt right, I'm ready.

Twenty-minutes later, Emily and I arrive at the decorated gymnasium after a companionable drive of small talk. This main gym is nicer than the one alumni games were relegated to earlier today, but the similar layout draws a satisfied smirk as I eye the bleachers. Emily must be thinking the same thing because an adorable flush reddens her skin.

Deciding to tease her a little, I step closer with the pretense of helping remove her coat and whisper, "It's darker in here, with only the fairy lights brightening the room. We can get away with a lot more if you're up for it."

"Under the bleachers again?" Her quiet murmur is barely audible over the music playing in the background. A while back, the alumni committee requested everyone's favorite songs from our time at Trinity College, so I'm guessing this playlist is the compilation of those responses as a poppy dance song fills the room.

A filthy idea bounces around my head. One I definitely shouldn't suggest when we're on uncertain ground, but this weekend's been filled with mistakes on my part, yet Emily's rolled with them. Perhaps she'll continue the trend.

"Not exactly. Why don't we say hello to everyone we need to before I share what I have in mind?" Figure starting slow and getting her comfortable might sway her to my side when the time comes.

Skepticism wrinkles her nose, but her friend Melanie saves me from answering any rebuttal she has.

"Hey, guys! Don't you make a cute couple?" The lithe redhead winks and leads us to a table full of people I recognize though wouldn't call close friends. Everyone welcomes me and Emily with giant smiles, and we chat about all the work done this weekend to set up events and the awards ceremony the next day. Apparently, this is the group of former student government alum, though they're missing their leader, Kenzie.

"I haven't seen her since the obstacle course yesterday." A man in black glasses admits, shrugging his shoulders. "There was a minor accident, but she seemed okay. So, I'm not sure why she's not here."

"Maybe she was worn out. She's had a busy weekend with organizing so much." Emily's voice softens in concern. Circling the back of her neck with my hand, I massage the tense muscles, hoping to soothe her. "I'll text her just to check-in."

The conversation moves on once Emily types out a message, and we stay a little longer before switching to hang out with my friends. It's nice sharing friend groups and melding our lives even in this small way. It shows that we're not so different. She gets along with my circle, and I get along with hers. No one feels so out of place that we could never work together.

But whatever happiness I feel pales in comparison to the anticipation in my gut as we're finally free to be alone. Separating from the crowd, we drift to the side of the gym underneath a banner welcoming everyone back to campus, and my mind whirs with the evening's possibilities.

However, Emily's phone buzzes with an incoming text, and the moment she reads the message, her face falls into the same resigned expression of sadness I saw at the cocktail dinner.

"What's wrong?"

She offers a weak smile before sighing and returning to her phone. "My reality check." Letters bounce across the screen as Emily's fingers type out a long response, her subdued demeanor a direct contrast to the positive glow she held earlier.

"What does that mean? How can I help?" Because I want to. Need to. At the cocktail party, I was stuck watching from afar, but we're together now—allowed to delve into each other's lives and do whatever we can to make it easier.

"You can't." She waves her phone through the air in frustration. A shaky hand runs through the long waves of hair she left loose for tonight. "I need to leave. I thought I could enjoy some casual fun. But this isn't fun. It reminds me of what I don't have, will probably never have, and I almost wish I didn't know what I was missing."

"This isn't casual," I deny.

Emily grimaces, ignoring me as she continues, "I warned you, you don't want any part of my life. I'm still dealing with the same drama I had ten years ago. Because I'm too weak to end the cycle. The rest of my life is bound to be shackled. Yours doesn't have to be."

"Come on." I grab her hand, pulling her towards a side exit. "We're not doing this here." The backdrop of happy people and loud music provides little privacy for a conversation we clearly need to have. Our feet shuffle across scuffed linoleum as we enter an empty hallway—my strides measured and determined while Emily hurries to keep up with me.

"Where are we going?" Another notification resonates from her phone, and I'm tempted to snatch it away and tell whoever's on the other side to leave Emily the hell alone.

A door appears on our left, so I try the knob and release a breath of gratitude as it turns. I usher Emily inside what turns out to be a locker room, flipping the metal lock to ensure no one bothers us before removing my jacket and tossing it on a wooden bench. Best to get comfortable while we wade into whatever mess she's trying to keep from me.

"What are we doing here?" she asks, pacing the row of metal lockers, arms crossed over her chest in a protective gesture.

"You're going to tell me what's going on, who's messaging you. And *together*," I stress the word, catching the slight pause in her step. "We'll figure out how to move forward because I meant it when I said I'm not giving you up. This isn't a random fling that ends tomorrow. You're mine, and I'm not dancing around that fact any longer. I won't let you deny it either."

Another message lights up her phone. *That's it.* Holding out my hand, I wait for her to drop the offending piece of metal and plastic into my palm. The screen's already unlocked, a barrage of messages stacked upon each other. Assuming her tacit agreement of me reading these texts since she gave me her phone willingly, I scroll through conversation after conversation of her parents demanding money, of her patiently asking questions—a couple of times even explaining how their constant financial demands made her feel—with no obvious remorse coming from her mom and dad.

Anger twists in my gut the further back I go, my grip tightening on the phone, threatening to crush it under my fury at how badly she's been treated. The messages end six months prior to today, but I know that's probably due to space constraints on the phone rather than the requests for money stopping.

Emily is the kindest, most generous person I've met—a genuinely good person. I recognized it in school, and I've seen it again this weekend with her choice to volunteer to make everyone else's reunion better instead of enjoying time with her own friends. It took me seconds to discover what a treasure she is.

Yet her shitty family hasn't figured it out, choosing to take advantage of her generous nature rather than protect it.

Yeah, that's not going to fly anymore—not if I have any say in the matter.

CHAPTER SIX

EMILY

Landon's quiet after giving my phone back. *Probably deciding how to retract all those promises of wanting more,* the fatalistic part of me bemoans. But best he knows what he's getting himself into now rather than later.

"You've been dealing with this by yourself for over ten years?" he finally asks, the muscles of his jaw constricting.

"I told you I can't stop the cycle. Despite therapy. Despite knowing how badly it affects me because they only reach out when they need something from me." The breath hitches in my lungs as tears threaten to spill over. "I can't say no without guilt or shame, so I give in."

"Oh, sweetheart." Landon wraps his arms around my waist, hugging tightly, and it breaks the dam of emotions I was saving for my pity party tomorrow. Resting my forehead on his chest, hot tears slide down my cheeks to seep into his shirt, dampening the white cotton.

"I've stressed about this weekend since deciding to come," I admit with a shaky voice. "Worrying about what terrible thing would happen while gone. Berating myself for wasting money on a trip." Landon squeezes harder in response—triggering more honesty at his steady kindness. "But I came anyway because I've lived with stress and anxiety for so long, I figured what's one weekend for myself? That's part of why I'm just kind of going with the flow with you. Because this weekend is for me, and I want to store up every good memory, want to let go of every worry before I return to reality. But, of course, I ruin it by letting them suck me in with their drama."

"You haven't ruined anything. The weekend's not over. Tonight's not over," he whispers in my ear. "I hate that you've carried this burden alone for so long, but you don't have to anymore. I'm not running. I'm not scared."

"And I'm supposed to believe you so easily? How? Why?"

"Because I used to be the burden in my family—the troubled kid." Landon loosens his grip enough to draw back and cup my face, brushing away stray tears. "I did what I wanted without caring how it affected my family. They always bailed me out of scrapes, adjusted their schedules to deal with whatever teacher conference or detention I had. Lived with my attitude throughout high school and part of college."

"That's supposed to make me feel better?" It's hard to imagine him being a troublemaker. As someone inconsiderate of others since he's been nothing but understanding and respectful this weekend.

"It's supposed to give you hope. I turned my life around, which means maybe your family can, too. But even if they don't change, I'll be right by your side because I understand what you're going through. You don't ever need to worry about me either, because I've matured. I know how to care for myself, and all I really want to do is care for you. There's nothing you need to do to earn my devotion."

Earnestness gleams from his green eyes, and I know he means it. He truly wants me for me.

Without overthinking it like I would.

Without doubting it like I am.

Just a man who knows his heart and his limits and is willing to risk them for me—Emily Houghton.

"Just like that." I snap my fingers. "You're all in."

"Yes."

I feel giddy. Nauseous. Nervous. An entire colony of roving emotions march through my body as his words sink in. If Melanie or any of my other friends told me about a guy declaring himself so openly to them, I'd push them so fast in his direction it would make their heads spin. And I know they'd do the same for me right now. Scream at me to stop being ridiculous. To stop being scared.

To trust for once.

To risk falling in love with a man who could end up breaking my heart. *Or protecting it for the rest of your lives together.*

Trust Landon. You can do it.

But is it right?

"Does it make me selfish to let you in, though? I feel like I'm taking advantage of you—using you," I admit, ever aware of needing to be good, to be kind, to make up for my family's flaws. "I've wished for someone to bear this burden with me for years, but I've also known how impossible it would be. It's been a dream I knew would never come true because I couldn't let another person be hurt like me."

"Emily, listen to me. You are the least selfish person I know. In fact, you're being overly accommodating if we're being honest, and that's something else we'll work on. Because it's not wrong for you to want someone to love you." He leans closer, ensuring I hear and believe every word he speaks. "You're not using how I feel as a power chip to get your way. I am freely offering myself to you. Are we clear?"

Yes.

Finally.

Covering his hands with my own, I nod. "We're clear. I'm going to follow your lead and see where it takes me because I'm tired of fighting this when I really don't want to. Denying this because it feels like I should to be a good person, not because it's what I really want."

"Good's overrated, right?" A tender smile lifts the corners of his mouth as he smooths a thumb over my bottom lip. "Which means it's time I dirtied you up. The rest of tonight will be spent with either my face, hand, or cock between your thighs, and there will be no more talk of drama or families or anything remotely sad." Landon snatches my phone back when it sounds again and turns it off before shoving it in his back pocket. "My original plans for the evening have shifted a bit, but we're going to make it work, aren't we, sweetheart?"

"Yes, we are." Tilting my head to the side, I glance around the locker room and decide it's time to show him my appreciation of his acceptance. To return the favor of the pleasure he gave me under the bleachers. Not to balance the scales, but because there's a need in me to be his in every way. "Starting with you sharing one of your fantasies with me. Surely, you've thought of some with how much time you've spent in here after practices and games."

"Tonight's about you, not me. We can discuss my fantasies later."

"But this is what I want," I press, hungry to learn what's lurking beneath his blonde façade, because him holding me by the throat yesterday? That felt intoxicating. And dangerous. His dark desire to corrupt me making my body slick with need. "Please, just tell me."

Landon groans, ruffling his hair with a shake of his head. "I'm not sure you're ready to hear mine. It's not very romantic."

I smile at the sweet sentiment. "It doesn't have to be."

His eyes drop to my chest, then raise to meet my curious gaze. Distant bass coming from the dance reverberates in the room as we stand across from each other, hovering on the edge of no return. Then the bubble of silence bursts, and we're catapulted forward as Landon growls. "I want to come on your tits. I want to fuck between their ample curves to completion. Until they're covered in my cum."

He's right. I wasn't ready to hear that. However, I'm not going to refuse him.

It sounds freaking hot. Like he's marking me as his in an elemental way—something that should bother me, I'm sure, but strangely just makes me more excited.

I like the idea of belonging to him. The love bite he left on my neck yesterday has caught my eye every time I've passed a mirror, despite Melanie helping me mask it with makeup. And if we're going to do this, then I'm going all in. I want to be branded as his in every way possible.

Time to make up for keeping myself at a distance from men and relationships.

Time to revel in being bad and let him dirty me beyond recognition.

CHAPTER SEVEN

LANDON

"**O**kay."

One word, and my world tilts on its axis.

Okay.

Emily pulls the zipper at the side of her dress down and allows the navy fabric to loosen then fall, leaving her standing in a lacy bra and panties. She toes off her shoes and steps out of the discarded gown, heading to a rack full of clean, folded towels, picking one up then dropping it to the tile at my feet before kneeling and looking up at me expectantly.

Am I dreaming?

In what reality does my dream girl kneel practically naked in front of me, waiting for directions?

Clearing my throat, I desperately grasp for composure as my cock presses against the front of my slacks. "That wild streak of yours goes deeper than I thought, sweetheart. Because this behavior's verging on very, very bad."

She smirks, and my temperature rises another ten degrees at how sexy she looks, satisfied with her small win over me. "Haven't you heard? Good girls are just bad girls who haven't been caught."

"Oh, make no mistake." My hands bury themselves in her hair and urge her forward until the heat of her breath ghosts over my trapped erection. "You're caught—good or bad—you're mine. Now, free me from these pants. You're gonna have to get me nice and wet before I can slide between those gorgeous tits of yours." Like a rabid wolf, I'm practically salivating at the image. From that first night I saw her in the rain, I've itched to glide between her breasts, to feel all that softness surround me. "Have you ever sucked a man's cock before, sweetheart?"

A whispered "no" floats upward as she works to release me from the confines of my clothing, the first graze of her fingers over my hard arousal making me jerk in response. Drops of pre-cum coat the tip of my cock, and I watch in fascination as Emily studies it with interest, her eyes creasing at the edges.

"What are you thinking?" I rasp out, using my grip on her hair to knead her scalp, hoping to soothe any doubts about her decision.

"A lot of things..." Emily stares up at me with an affectionate smile. "What to do first... I hope I do this right..." Then her expression slightly dims. "Have you done this here with other girls...?"

"Absolutely not. I wouldn't disrespect you that way. Most of the time I spent in this locker room was with the guys after a game or practice, and my mind was preoccupied with how I played or what I should have done differently. I didn't care to hang out here when it wasn't necessary." Sweeping a thumb over her cheek, I add, "You're the only woman I've ever thought about while in here. And you're definitely the only one I plan on fucking in here."

Her shoulders visibly relax as she sighs. "Thank you. I don't begrudge your past, but I hate the idea of being compared and..."

"That's not an issue. You're the only woman in my mind and in my future. Past affairs are over and forgotten because they don't hold a candle to you. They never have, which is why they never lasted."

Emily's hand palms my cock in a hesitant grip before she kisses the tip, creating a sheen of cum on her lips as a low sound of acceptance hums in her throat. Her hand clasps tighter around my erection, stroking me from base to tip as if testing the length and girth, before dropping her jaw and drawing an open kiss along the underside, her tongue leaving behind a wet trail.

I rest one hand on the line of lockers behind me as my weight falls backward, weak from Emily's slow exploration. I want to rush her. I want to slide between those pouty pink lips until I feel her throat struggle to swallow me deeper. I want her face shiny with saliva and cum to match what'll happen to her tits.

But tenderness keeps a harsh grip on my lust.

Emily's new to this. She's sweet and innocent and *good*. She deserves a chance to learn at her own pace and please me in her gentle way.

We have our entire lives for the rest of it, I tell myself. Because I'm not going to ruin this for her.

"I like the way you taste. Is that weird?"

"Hell, no. I'm glad you like it because I fucking love the way you taste." The delicious teaser I had yesterday after I licked my fingers clean of her essence has me thirsty for more.

"Oh... Good..." A shy flush heats her skin before she ducks her head—whatever fear she had alleviated because her lips wrap around the tip of my cock and suck enthusiastically. With the barest guidance of my hand in her hair, she finds a rhythm, pushing her limits with each swallow, until I recognize the signs of my impending climax and urge her away.

She starts to protest but stops once I'm positioned on one of the locker room benches and wave her forward. "Alright, sweetheart, show me what that gorgeous body of yours can do," I dare, allowing her to prove how good she is—catnip for my girl.

Wasting no time, Emily readjusts herself on the folded towel under her knees and shimmies close enough to guide my glistening cock to her chest. Midnight blue lace cups the heavy globes lovingly, and the aroused points of her nipples are obvious through the thin fabric.

"Like this?" She pushes her breasts together, forming a snug passage for my cock, and rubs them up and down.

"Yeah, just like that." I grunt, white knuckling the wooden bench. "You should never wear anything but lingerie and my cum. Fuck, do you know how sexy you look"

"Probably not as sexy as this." A cheeky grin appears, then a hot swipe of her tongue registers as she engulfs the head of my cock in her mouth. Insistent suckling follows as she increases the pressure surrounding my hard-on.

"Mmm... you're right. But since you want to make this a competition." I ease her back with one hand as another replaces her touch on my dick, jerking it roughly until splashes of white cum drench her chest, dripping down the deep valley created by her bra. Satisfaction settles deep in my bones—the first true sense of relaxation I've felt all weekend.

Emily's mine.

And when she coyly dips a finger into the mess I've made, sucking it off her delicate skin with a moan of pleasure, I know she's mine forever.

Because my good girl's also a hell of a dirty girl, and I'm the only man who'll ever know the truth.

CHAPTER EIGHT

EMILY

I'm not sure what's come over me, but I love it.

It's empowering to witness Landon's loss of control and know I'm the reason for it. Me—a virgin—*fucked* him with my breasts, sucked on his cock, and I want to do it again. I want to do more.

There's freedom in understanding Landon's attention isn't conditional.

He's not using me for personal gain.

Heck, he's nursed a crush for a decade with nothing but a vision of me soaked from the rain and an awkward lunch conversation. And for no other reason than he likes me as I am.

The relief it brings, the sheer enormity of such a priceless gift, is overwhelming.

Landon leans forward for a kiss that rapidly escalates into me climbing into his lap like a spider monkey, uncaring about my weight or if he can hold me—my focus centered on imprinting myself on him. As he rips off his dress shirt, I undo the hooks of my bra, allowing it to join his discarded shirt on the worn tile. We both moan at the slick slide of our chests against one other, his cum easing the friction, the light whorls of hair covering hard pectorals teasing my nipples.

"I can taste myself on your tongue." The possessive tone of satisfaction gets lost in another harsh kiss, Landon devouring me in greedy bites and licks. "You've got me twisted up inside, Em. I had plans to eat your cunt until you begged for mercy. Remember how I promised to lick every inch of you?"

I manage a controlled nod and groan, grinding against the growing erection between my legs. He just came, yet Landon's apparently ready for a second round—one I'm all too happy to give him because I ache inside. I need to know what it's like to be filled by him.

To give myself entirely to him.

"Except now all I can think about is feeling your hot pussy choke my dick until I'm pumping you full of cum. Is that alright, sweetheart?" he asks as if I really have a choice when his hand tugs the lace of my panties aside, notching the mushroom head of his cock at the opening of my pussy. "I'll make it up to you, I swear. Tomorrow, you'll wake up with my face buried in your cunt. I'll spell out my apology on your sweet clit with every drag of my tongue."

His fingers dig into my bottom, pressing bruises of ownership into the pale skin, and the low rumble of Landon's voice sends a shiver down my spine. "Be my good girl and ride me. Be my dirty girl and force my cum to coat your cunt and drip down your thighs. So, when we leave tonight, you're sticky and sore, with no doubt in your mind of who you belong to."

"Is this the part where I say, *Yes, sir*?" I joke half-heartedly, a part of me thrilled by the prospect. Forty-eight hours ago, I never would've imagined I'd be sitting on Landon's lap in one of Trinity's locker rooms, covered in his cum and hoping for more.

He really is a miracle worker. *Or I was really repressed.* A dark shot of humor flits through my mind.

A decade of stress and anxiety will do that to a person, I suppose. But thank goodness for this reunion.

It's shown me the possibility of a new future—one where a man loves and accepts me as I am, heavy baggage and all.

He hasn't said "I love you" yet.

But he will. I know it.

"Say whatever you want, sweetheart. As long as it's while my cock's inside your pretty pussy." His hands urge me forward, and I follow the wordless command, sinking down until my clit rubs against his pelvis.

Full of Landon and strangely enough, amusement, I nip at his ear with a mocking "Yes, sir" muttered into his skin. My knees slip along the wooden bench with each bounce of my hips, impaling myself on the steel cock colliding with my G-spot on every plunge.

My array of hidden sex toys at home seems lackluster compared to this. There's something about having a sturdy man beneath me, someone to hold on to and who's holding me, that feels like the joy of chocolate, getting an A, and having a girls' night all wrapped into one pure shot of pleasure.

I never want it to end.

A shock of warmth pulls on my nipple as Landon suckles the stiff peak, distracting me. "You and I are the perfect mix," he says, and the taboo nature of him tasting his own cum on my breast sends me into oblivion. The rhythm of my movements becomes stuttered as my muscles contract in unison, releasing the built-up sexual tension of this weekend.

Landon helps me through it, his thumb lowering to circle my clit while he continues to thrust upward, until his own climax takes over, and we're both left sweating and shuddering in the quiet locker room.

"I'm not sure how we're gonna top this at the next reunion." The ridiculous statement causes an eruption of breathless laughter before we disentangle ourselves to stand on wobbly legs.

"I'm sure you'll think of something," I say, grinning before picking up the displaced towel on the floor and tossing it in a large hamper along the wall. With each step, Landon's vow to leave me sticky and sore comes true as his cum drips down my inner thighs. And it occurs to me we didn't use protection.

Wow, when you decide to go bad, you go all in.

Quickly getting dressed, I wait for Landon to finish retying his shoes before broaching the topic. "So... we didn't use a condom. And I'm not on birth control since I've never really needed it."

He pauses and glances up at me. "And we just had sex."

I bite my lip as my chin bobs up and down.

A tenderness darkens the green of his eyes as he stands and wraps me in a firm hug. "Whatever happens, we'll deal with it together. Whether you're pregnant or not. I'm not leaving you, Emily. You belong to me. Understand?"

Breathing a sigh of relief, the corners of my lips lift in a slight smile. "Yes. We'll deal with it together."

Landon lets loose a bright grin of delight before taking my hand and leading me outside. We bypass the gym where the dance is still going strong, wordlessly agreeing to call it a night as far as socializing with others goes.

"Happy to hear you're learning, sweetheart. Because together is how we'll handle the rest of our lives, including any baby surprises and your family."

And that sounds perfect to me.

EPILOGUE ONE

LANDON
ONE YEAR LATER

S *weet as honey.*

The wet sound from eating Emily's pussy beneath the covers is my favorite melody, and one I play every morning after promising to wake her with my mouth our first night together. She likes to hem and haw, insisting it's unnecessary for me to make up for reneging on the commitment I made last year at our reunion, but deep down, I know my girl loves every second my tongue laps at her clit.

"Mmm, good morning..." The sleepy moan drifts from above as Emily stretches, her legs widening to give me better access.

"Morning, sweetheart. Did you sleep well?" I continue to stroke her with my fingers, so I can drop a kiss on her waiting mouth, relishing the sight of her pink lips damp with her own arousal.

"Mhmm... I think the melatonin actually worked." Though I support Emily, however I can, she still struggles with worry over her family. They haven't changed much in the past year, and the façade of a perfect family that they'd put on at our first meeting quickly dissolved once they realized I was going to put up with their bullshit. Or allow it to touch Emily anymore.

To the extent that she'll let me, that is.

We're working with a therapist to guide her through her guilt and shame for the sense that she's abandoning them by not financially supporting them. But it takes time to unlearn years' worth of trauma and habits, so I do what I can, though to my frustration, it's not always enough.

Like her current sleeping problems because her mom's been messaging about money for a car of her own.

"I'm glad. Together, the melatonin and I are going to kick your insomnia's ass." I blow a raspberry against her neck as she laughs, then moans when my fingers hit a particularly sensitive spot in her pussy.

"I have complete faith in you."

Love wells in my chest, an emotion that deepens every day. Emily's put so much trust in me. From the day we met at our ten-year reunion. To the moment we found out she wasn't pregnant after our first time together. She's overcome a lot of her fear and doubts—a courageous woman whom I adore.

"As you should." I plant playful kisses from her lips to the valley between her breasts, then over her round belly before returning to my previous spot between her legs. Another giggle melts into a moan as Emily wriggles beneath me, lifting her hips to entice me into a faster pace, but I refuse to rush.

I hum against her clit, knowing how much the gentle vibration heightens her arousal. I've learned so many little details about Emily over the past twelve months, especially since I decided to move closer to her. My friends supported me, though my coworkers thought I was crazy for quitting my job and moving across the country for a woman.

But I haven't regretted a moment of it.

I got my dream girl.

The good girl who fulfills my every fantasy.

And as Emily's cry of elation follows the hot release of her climax, I bury my satisfied grin in her pussy, eager for more.

After all, my girl's meant to be savored.

EPILOGUE TWO

EMILY
NINE YEARS LATER

I close the door with a sigh and lean against the smooth grain, smiling at Landon, as the excited chatter of our children fades with the slamming of their grandparents' car door. "Well, we've got an entire weekend to ourselves. Are you ready?"

"Always." His strong arms wrap around my waist before dropping a kiss on my forehead. "Though we could skip the reunion and spend the next few days in bed." I know he's only half-serious—Josh and Maggie would kill us for not showing up at our twentieth college reunion at Trinity.

Over the years, Maggie has turned into a surrogate sister to me, and our families have shared numerous vacations together, something I never would've foreseen for myself. A normal life filled with supportive friends who've become family. And in-laws who've acted as better parents than my own.

It took me a long time with Landon's help, along with a therapist, to finally cut my parents off. The toxic drama of our relationship never changed despite my pleas for improvement, baring my pain in an effort to make them see how badly I've been affected. But they didn't care. Only saw themselves as the victims, going so far as to blame Landon for turning me against them.

So, I did the hardest thing I've ever done in my life—stopped all communication with them.

That was a difficult time.

But Landon's parents, who'd moved nearer to us after I had our first child, Gwen, took me in and showed me what unconditional love from a mom and dad could look like. Nurturing and kind, I could see where Landon inherited some of his best traits.

"Tempting, but think about all the fun we had at our ten-year reunion," I tease. "Surely, there's some other spot on campus you want to *corrupt* me in?" It's become our thing for him to steal me away at the most inappropriate times to *dirty me up*, and I love every second of it.

"Hmmm... You're right. The library has definite possibilities."

Laughing at his predictability, I pat his chest before pushing him away to finish packing for our trip. "Exactly. Did you remember to add Gwen's unicorn pillow to her travel bag? Otherwise, she's going to throw a fit when she realizes it's missing."

"Would I forget to make sure one of my favorite girls has everything she needs?"

No, he wouldn't.

Because Landon takes better care of us than I ever would have imagined.

Despite maturing and getting his life together long before we fell in love, his parents like to tease about the good effect I have on him while regaling me with all the sordid stories of his past. We joke about it now, but I know those times were hard for their family.

Pausing on the stairs, I turn around and find myself eye to eye with Landon, our height difference negated for once. "No, you wouldn't, and I love you for it." I carefully press a kiss to his lips, bracing my hands on his shoulders for stability.

"I love you, too, sweetheart." He deepens the embrace until somehow, we end up on the carpeted landing a couple steps up, and my blouse is fluttering open to give him access to the soft mounds of my breasts. Throughout two pregnancies, he's adored my body, lavishing each added stretch mark and roll of flesh with kisses and words of love—and today's no different.

"Fuck, I love you so much. All I want to do is worship you day and night." A reverential lick dips below one of my bra cups to lap at a sensitive nipple while his hand squeezes a love handle that's overflowed the waist of my jeans. "You're my home, my temple, and I never want to lose you."

"You won't," I promise, caressing his blonde waves. "Because you're my home, too." Drawing his head higher, our mouths meet in a melding of heat and commitment—an affirmation of what's been and what's to come.

And everything else fades until it's just the two of us: a former playboy basketball player and his good girl.

Who's only bad with him, the love of my life.

Don't miss Kenzie's story in Campus Queen!

Avoid heartbreak at all costs.
Kenzie Beechman prefers being in charge. Life's taught her that she's the only one she can count on and risking herself again is out of the question. When her ex-boyfriend arrives at their ten-year college reunion happily married to someone else, it's a stark reminder of how little control she's had over her love life. Could a former classmate's offer of a guilt-free fling be just the distraction she needs?

Until a man from her past offers to distract her for the weekend in more pleasurable ways...

Joel Beecham was a slacker and part-time class clown. Partnered with Kenzie on multiple school projects, he never pulled his weight. But a decade of life changes a man and Joel's ready to apologize for his mistakes and make amends...in bed. He proposes a homecoming affair with one caveat—Kenzie must submit to him in the bedroom.

With only a few days together, can casual fun turn into a forever kind of love?

CAMPUS QUEEN *features a curvy girl who strives for perfection and the dirty-talking man who frees her to be herself—flaws and all. A short & steamy romance for those who've wondered **What If...?***

TROPES INCLUDED: *Instalove, Type A Girl/Slacker Guy, Forced Proximity, Weekend Fling, Dominant in the Sheets/Beta on the Streets, Let's Make a Deal, & Curvy Heroine*

THANKS FOR READING & DON'T FORGET TO RATE/ REVIEW!

Please consider leaving a rating/review on Amazon, Goodreads, Instagram, TikTok, and/or any other sites you review on.
Ratings & reviews are the #1 way to support an indie author like me.
They don't have to be long or even positive (though I hope you enjoyed this book!). All the algorithms care about are QUANTITY.
The more reviews, the more my books are shown to other potential readers!
And they serve as guides to readers on whether or not to take a chance on an indie author.
Also, don't miss out on free books and up-to-date release information. You can sign up for my newsletter here.
I appreciate your support!
XO, Hallie

ABOUT THE AUTHOR

Hallie prefers steamy, insta-love stories where curvy girls are claimed by filthy-talking heroes. And when she ran out of reading material, she decided to write her own stories. If you want a quick, hot read, she's your girl!